This is a monkey puzzle tree, a member of a millennial species, thousands of years old.
Today, people use the word *millennial* to describe the generation that has grown up at
the beginning of the second millennium, or second thousand years of the Common Era.
But in this book we use the original meaning of *millennial*—a thousand.

A Small History of a Disagreement

First published in Spanish by Ediciones Ekaré Sur in 2017
Text copyright © 2017 by Claudio Fuentes S.
Illustrations copyright © 2017 by Gabriela Lyon
English translation copyright © 2020 by Elisa Amado
First published in Canada and the U.S. in 2020, and in the U.K. in 2021 by Greystone Books.

20 21 22 23 24 5 4 3 2 1

Greystone Kids / Greystone Books Ltd.
greystonebooks.com

An Aldana Libros book

Cataloguing data available from Library and Archives Canada
ISBN 978-1-77164-707-6 (cloth)
ISBN 978-1-77164-708-3 (epub)

Copy editing by Linda Pruessen
Proofreading by Elizabeth McLean
Jacket illustration by Gabriela Lyon
Printed and bound in China on ancient-forest-friendly paper by 1010 Printing International Ltd.

Greystone Books gratefully acknowledges the Musqueam, Squamish, and Tsleil-Waututh peoples
on whose land our office is located.

Greystone Books thanks the Canada Council for the Arts, the British Columbia Arts Council,
the Province of British Columbia through the Book Publishing Tax Credit, and the Government
of Canada for supporting our publishing activities.

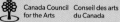

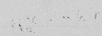

A SMALL HISTORY of a DISAGREEMENT

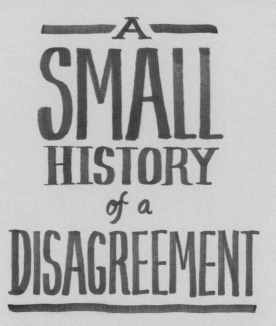

Claudio Fuentes S.

Illustrations by Gabriela Lyon

Translated by Elisa Amado

AN ALDANA LIBROS BOOK

GREYSTONE KIDS

GREYSTONE BOOKS • VANCOUVER / BERKELEY

That Monday, when we came back to school after
the holidays, there was a surprise waiting for us.

A huge crane filled the sky and a rough wooden fence was blocking the schoolyard.

"Hey! And this? What's this?" we asked each other.

Somebody said they'd heard that the developers were going to cut down the monkey puzzle tree to build a new building. "Cut it down?" a bunch of kids said in shocked voices. "A building? What for?"

During that first recess, kids pushed up against the fence.

Someone had written, "Don't cut down the monkey puzzle tree. It's millennial."

Some kids began yelling, "Millennial! Millennial!"

Soon, more joined in. "MIL-LEN-NI-AL! MIL-LEN-NI-AL!"

The playground monitor got pretty nervous. He tried to impose order.

There were two "millennial" days like that.

Then the principal called the whole school to an urgent meeting. She explained that it was about a redevelopment project. She showed us plans and drawings. The construction of a new building would, without a doubt, bring progress and development to the school—new classrooms, science laboratories, a computer lab. But we'd lose the main schoolyard... and the monkey puzzle tree.

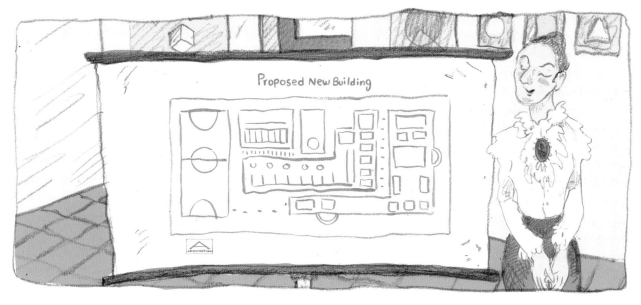

Suddenly, alongside chants of "MIL-LEN-NI-AL!" we started to hear "DE-VE-LOP-MENT! DE-VE-LOP-MENT!"

At first the voices were kind of timid, but then they got louder.

Thursday morning, there was a huge poster hanging on the monkey puzzle tree.

Somehow or other, a new message appeared every day.

During the night Millennials had jumped over the school fence and sneakily hung them up. The people who wanted the new building said, "If they are Millennials, we are Developers," and they also began to hang up posters and banners. One bunch of kids protested one day, another the next. And sometimes, everyone was at it all at once. There were so many protests that the principal decided to call another meeting.

"The best way to solve problems is to talk to each other and listen," she said.

Everyone yelled at once: "Millennials!" "Developers!"

The history teacher spoke up in an even louder voice. "We know that some students are against the construction of this building, and that others are in favor of it."

Bit by bit the shouts died down, and the teacher continued. "I propose we hold a debate where we can all state our positions. For that, everyone needs to think carefully about the arguments they can make for their side. Let's say this will be an exercise in civics."

The principal said, "Hmm... it might be interesting."

And we thought, "Ugh. That sounds like work."

We went to the library; we looked on the internet; we even asked some teachers.

Most of all, we sat down to talk and think in small groups.

MILLENNIALS
for nature

- The monkey puzzle tree was declared a National Monument in 1976 according to law #249.

- The monkey puzzle tree is a vulnerable species. We should respect and protect it!

- We need spaces to play and relax and spread out in a natural setting.

- The monkey puzzle tree is part of our millennial inheritance, and it connects us to the Mapuche people.

- Montuafiyiñ ta pewen! It means, "Save the monkey puzzle tree!"

At the end of the week the Millennials got together in one of the classrooms and prepared their arguments for the debate. In another room, the Developers did the same.

The Mapuche are one of the Indigenous peoples of Chile.

DEVELOPERS

FOR SCIENCE

- THE CONSTRUCTION OF THIS BUILDING WILL ALLOW US: NEW AND BETTER CLASSROOMS, LABORATORIES, MUSIC ROOMS, AND COMPUTER LABS.

- THE BUILDING REPRESENTS PROGRESS: MORE SCIENCE AND INNOVATION.

- THE SCHOOL NEEDS TO MODERNIZE SO ITS STUDENTS CAN AS WELL.

- ACCORDING TO LAW #299, "THE CUTTING OF A MONKEY PUZZLE TREE IS PERMITTED WHEN PREPARING LAND FOR THE CONSTRUCTION OF PUBLIC WORKS".

The debate was great, and the kids who were undecided
began to lean toward one side or the other.

The Developers made strong, rational arguments.

The Millennials' passion lit many people's hearts on fire.

We were all very excited. Someone asked the history teacher, "Shouldn't we have a vote?"

The teacher agreed right away. "Yes," he said, "a vote would be the best way to know how many are in favor and how many against.

We can hold a plebiscite, and vote 'yes' or 'no' to the new building."

The principal wasn't sure, but finally she said, "Hmm...it might be interesting."

Then the campaigns began!

We painted signs. We hung posters. We handed out flyers.
And we went on social media.

Almost everyone, even the shyest kids, had an opinion.
And almost the whole school participated. Nothing like
this had ever happened before.

We built booths and created ballot boxes. We made lists of who was
in each class and of all the people who worked at the school. Teachers,
assistants, cleaners, students—everybody had a right to vote.

Finally, after a very intense week, voting day arrived.

We had to answer the question:

Are you in favor of cutting down the monkey puzzle tree
to make room for the new building?

Mark *YES* or *NO* on the ballot.

It was a long day, but by the end of the afternoon the counting of the ballots began.

We were so nervous! Who would win? The Millennials? The Developers?

At six o'clock the principal picked up the microphone. For a few seconds she was silent. Then she spoke. "It's curious!" she said. "After counting and recounting all the ballots, we can confirm that the vote is tied."

Tied???!!!

So now...

what would we do?

The principal suggested another round of voting, a new campaign.

"Noooo!"

No one wanted that. We were all so tired!

"I understand," she said. "It's been a very challenging process, but maybe, hmm…
 very interesting, don't you think?"

Right at that moment, NO, we didn't think so.

Still, as days went by, we began to think about what might be "interesting."

Deciding "no" isn't simple, and neither is finding a solution. But disagreeing hadn't made us enemies. Instead, we'd actually gotten to know each other better. Someone even said that good ideas could come out of the disagreements.

And even more important, because of the vote, we knew that half the school wanted the building and the other half didn't.

That showed us a way...

Dear Principal,

With respect to your request, we are sending modified plans for the school's new building.
We hope you will appreciate the integration of the monkey puzzle tree into the design.
We look forward to your approval to begin construction.

Sincerely,

Peter Uribe
Architect

Modified Building Plan

Tree integrated into new building

ARQUITECTURA

After everything that happened at the school with the monkey puzzle tree and the building, the history teacher was still all excited and energetic.

He wrote on the blackboard:

- What is freedom of speech and how can we exercise it?
- How can we make sure everyone has a chance to express his or her opinion?
- Why bother voting?

"That's your assignment," he said.

Oh well, now we had our work cut out for us!

About the Monkey Puzzle Tree

Monkey puzzle trees are millennial.

Araucaria araucana — the scientific name for the monkey puzzle tree — is, in fact, a very ancient species, and one of the hardiest evergreen trees. But it is also endangered. It is native to central and southern Chile and western Argentina, where it has protected status. Its survival in the wild is threatened by logging, fires, invasive species, and other forces that are decimating great swaths of the native forests in the southern Andean region.

Because they are so interesting to look at, *Araucaria araucana* have been used as decorative trees in many parts of the world. In 1850, an Englishman, Sir William Molesworth, was showing off his new tree to his friends. One of them said, "It would puzzle a monkey to climb that."

Ever since, it has been called the monkey puzzle tree in English.

Claudio Fuentes S. holds a PhD in Political Science from the University of North Carolina. He is the author of numerous books and articles on issues concerning democratization, security, and international relations. He lives in Santiago de Chile, Chile.

Gabriela Lyon is a children's book illustrator, author, and teacher of drawing at Finis Terra University in Santiago de Chile.

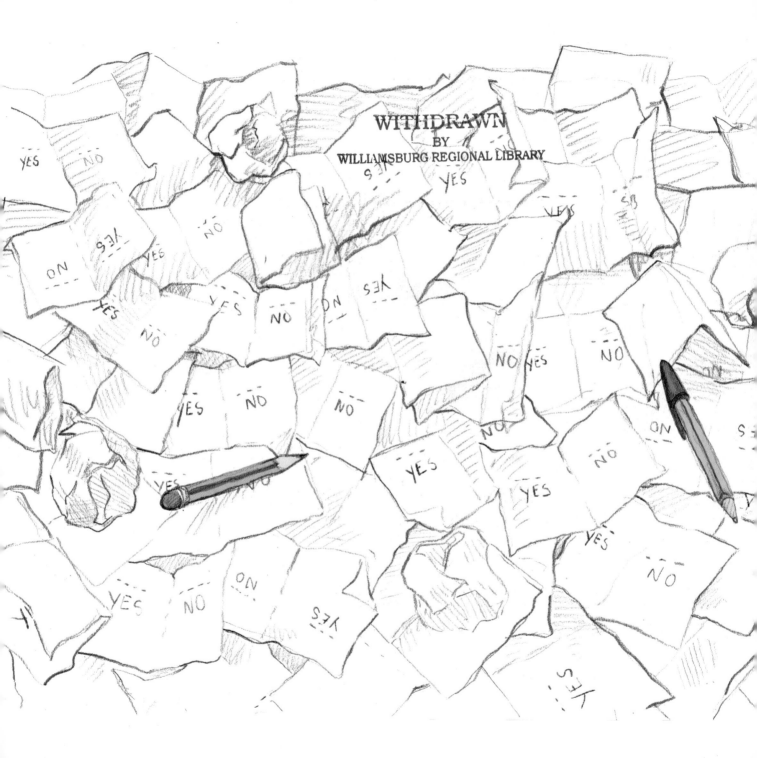